Happy I'm a Hippo

By Richard Edwards

Illustrated by Carol Liddiment

ALISON GREEN BOOKS

There was once a young hippo who didn't like being a hippo.

"I don't **like** being a hippo," she said to her friends.

"Why not?" they asked.

"Hippos are boring," said the young one.

"We just lie in the river or wallow in mud. Look at that cheetah run!
Look at that antelope jump! All we do is laze."

One morning, she waded out of the river . . .

"Where are you going, Hippo?" called the others.

"Don't call me hippo!" she said. "I've told you before.
I don't want to be a hippo!" And she turned her back on
her friends and stomped away.

The path was dusty and the day was hot,
but the hippo sang as she walked along:

"Don't want to be a hippo. No! No! No!
Rather be a zebra or a buffa-luffa-lo.
Rather be that monkey, swinging in his tree,
Rather be a monkey than a hippo like me."

"Hallo, Hippo!" called the monkey.

"Don't call me hippo!" said the hippo.

"Hippos are boring. I want to be a monkey,

exploring the treetops like you."

The monkey looked surprised.

"But, Hippo," he said:

"Can you swing along the branches?
Can you leap from tree to tree?
Can you dangle
by your tail?
Can you climb like me!"

"I can try!" said the hippo.

But hippos aren't made for climbing, and when
she tried to scramble up, the tree swayed and
the branches snapped and she
fell in a heap
on the
ground.

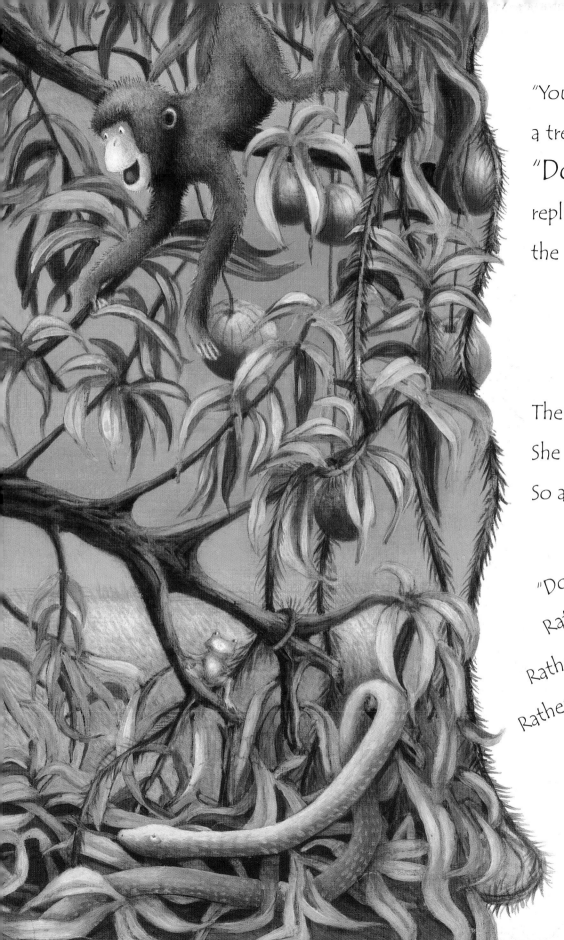

"You can't be a monkey if you can't climb a tree," the monkey said. "Sorry, Hippo."
"Don't call me hippo!" the hippo replied, as she crunched away through the broken sticks.

The sun grew hotter as the hippo walked on. She had so wanted to be a monkey.
So again she sang:

"Don't want to be a hippo. No! No! No!
Rather be a zebra or a buffa-luffa-lo.
Rather be that eagle, flying so free,
Rather be an eagle than a hippo like me."

"Hallo, Hippo!" the eagle called down.

"Don't call me hippo!" said the hippo.
"Hippos are **boring** and **clumsy**.
I want to be an eagle like you."

"Like me!" said the eagle in surprise.
"But, Hippo:

"Can you soar between the clouds?
Can you wheel and swoop and fly?
Can you flap and glide and circle
In the clear blue sky?"

"I can try!" the hippo answered.

But hippos aren't made for flying, and when
she ran down a slope and jumped to take off
she fell flat on her face with a

thump!

"You can't be an eagle if you can't fly,"
said the eagle. "Sorry, Hippo."

"Don't call me hippo!" said the hippo.

The day got hotter, and the sun beat fiercely
down. Back at the river the other hippos
would be wallowing in the cool mud.
But the young hippo didn't want to think
about that, so instead she sang:

"Don't want to be a hippo. No! No! No!
Rather be a zebra or a buffa-luffa-lo.
Rather be that meerkat, digging happily,
Rather be a meerkat than a hippo like me."

"Hallo, Hippo!" said the meerkat.

"Don't call me hippo!" said the hippo.

"Hippos are boring and clumsy and slow.

I want to be a meerkat like you."

"Really?" said the meerkat.

"But, Hippo:

"Can you scamper?
Can you skip?

Can you peer right round?

Can you scurry? Can you burrow
Down into the ground?"

"I can try!" said the hippo.

But hippos aren't made for burrowing, and when she tried
to dig she just scooped up a **huge** cloud of sand
that made her sneeze:

"Atchoo!"

"You can't be a meerkat if you can't dig a hole," said the meerkat. "Sorry, Hippo."

"Don't call me hippo!" the hippo whispered wearily as she trudged away.

The sun was at its hottest now, making her skin burn and her head ache and throb. She was beginning to feel she could hardly go one step further when she saw something glitter through the trees. At the bottom of a slope was a big muddy pool.

It was a water hole!

As she moved forward she saw a young wildebeest that had strayed
from his herd, approaching the pool on thin and wobbly legs.
He lowered his head and began to drink thirstily.
Nearby, something moved in the water . . .

A tree trunk in the pool was floating closer . . .

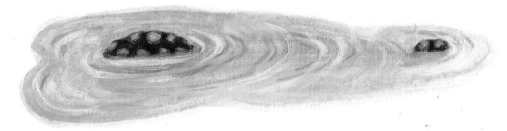

And closer . . .

Then it opened an eye . . .

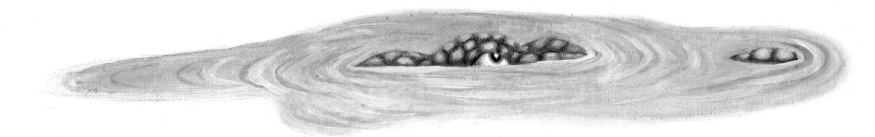

And opened another eye . . .

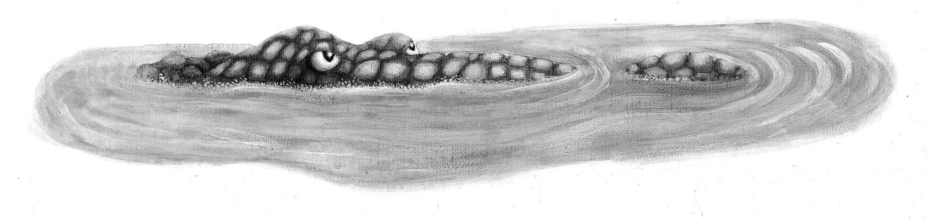

And opened its mouth in a toothy grin . . .

It wasn't a tree trunk at all: it was a hungry

crocodile!

"No!" cried the hippo.

Charging down the slope,
she plunged into the water and
made a huge wave that swept the crocodile away
to the other end of the pool.

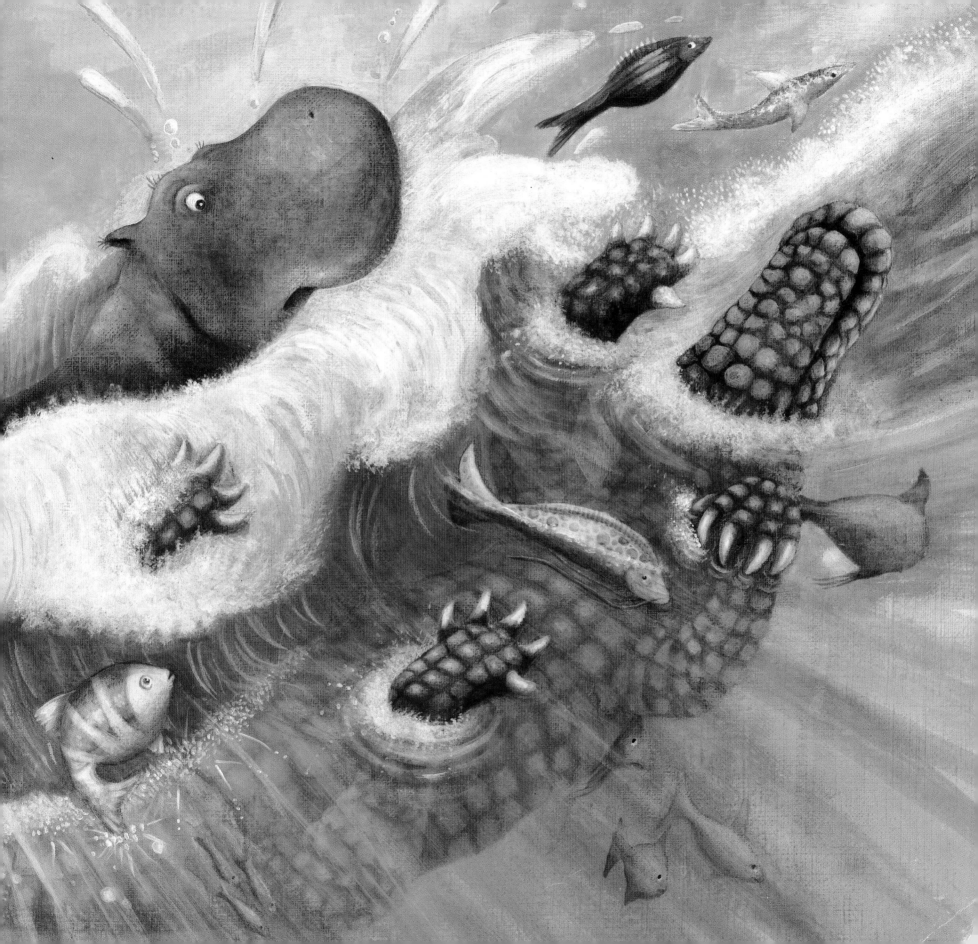

"Oh, **thank you**," said the wildebeest.

"You saved my life, Hippo!"

"Please don't call me that," said the hippo.

"I don't **want** to be a hippo."

"But, Hippo," said the wildebeest:

"You're so **lucky** being a hippo,
You can keep so **cool**,
You can **swim**, you can **dive**,
You can **wallow** in a pool.

"You're so **lucky** being a hippo,
You can **scare crocs**, too.
Oh, I **wish** I was a hippo
And as **big** and **brave** as you."

"Me, lucky?" said the hippo.

"Very lucky," the wildebeest replied.

"And brave, too?"

"Very brave. Very, very brave."

The little wildebeest went tottering back to his herd, and
the hippo smiled. It was good to be a hippo! And the next thing,
she was trotting home as fast as she could.

It was a long,
hot journey back.
Her skin was cracked and sunburned,
her mouth was dry and her feet ached.

At last she saw the river ahead!

She ran forward and plunged into the water
with a huge, loud splash!

It was so, so cool!

Lifted and rocked by the water, the young hippo felt light and clean and happier than ever to be back with her friends.

"Welcome back, Hippo!" said one.
"Don't call her hippo!" said another.
"She doesn't like being a hippo."
"That was before," the young hippo answered. "Now I can't think of anything better . . .

"Hippo!" shouted her friends, as she ducked under the surface

and came up grinning. Her friends grinned, too.

Such happy grins!

Such happy hippos!

For my sons, Robert and George – C.L.

First published in the UK in 2007 by
Alison Green Books
An imprint of Scholastic Children's Books
Euston House, 24 Eversholt Street
London NW1 1DB, UK
A division of Scholastic Ltd
London – New York – Toronto – Sydney – Auckland
Mexico City – New Delhi – Hong Kong

HB 10-digit ISBN: 0 439 95028 7
HB 13-digit ISBN: 978 0 439950 28 2
PB 10-digit ISBN: 0 439 94437 6
PB 13-digit ISBN: 978 0 439944 37 3

Text copyright © 2007 Richard Edwards
Illustrations copyright © 2007 Carol Liddiment
All rights reserved.

1 3 5 7 9 8 6 4 2

Printed in Singapore

For my lovely sister, Anita xxx
L.P.

For Evie and her mummy and daddy xxx
C.P.

First published 2018 by Nosy Crow Ltd
The Crow's Nest, 14 Baden Place
Crosby Row, London SE1 1YW
www.nosycrow.com

ISBN 978 1 78800 265 3 (HB)
ISBN 978 1 78800 266 0 (PB)

Nosy Crow and associated logos are trademarks
and/or registered trademarks of Nosy Crow Ltd.

Text © Lou Peacock 2018
Illustrations © Christine Pym 2018

The rights of Lou Peacock to be identified as the author and of
Christine Pym to be identified as the illustrator of this work have been asserted.

A CIP catalogue record for this book is available from the British Library.

Printed in China by Imago

Papers used by Nosy Crow are made from wood grown in sustainable forests.

10 9 8 7 6 5 4 3 2 1 (HB)
10 9 8 7 6 5 4 3 2 1 (PB)

Toby
and the
Tricky Things

Lou Peacock &
Christine Pym

nosy crow

Toby knew that
he was getting bigger.

He thought he might
be a **Big Boy**.

He could pour
his own milk.

He could read his own
bedtime stories.

He could even reach the snacks that Mummy said were "just for mummies".

In fact, he could do most things **All By Himself**. Being a **Big Boy**, thought Toby, was **marvellous**.

He was also bigger than
his little sister, Iris.

Iris was very,
very small.

And because Iris was **so** small,
Mummy was very busy.

And this meant that, sometimes,
Toby had to do the **Tricky Things**
All By Himself.

The **Tricky Things,** Toby had to admit,
were still **Tricky,** even though
he was a **Big Boy.**

When Toby had to do up his buttons,
Mummy was too busy with Iris to help.

"I'm just putting Iris's hat on, Toby," she said.
"But you're my Big Boy. You can do things All By Yourself."

But Toby couldn't.
Those buttons really were **Too Tricky.**
And he had **Bad Buttons** all day.

When Toby had to put on his wellies,
Mummy was still too busy with Iris to help.

"I'm just settling Iris in her pram, Toby," she said.
"But you're my Big Boy. You can do things All By Yourself."

But Toby couldn't.
Those wellies really were
Too Tricky. And he had
Wrong Wellies all day.

OPEN

And when it came to that
other **Tricky Thing,**
it all went very wrong indeed.

Toby began to wonder
if being a **Big Boy** wasn't
so marvellous after all.

He called for Mummy . . .

And Mummy fixed the **Tricky Things!**
"Mummy," said Toby, "pants and
loo paper are **Tricky Things**
and I can't do **Tricky Things**
All By Myself."

"Toby, you are such a **Big Boy** and you
can do all sorts of things **All By Yourself,**"
said Mummy, "but I am always here
to help with the **Tricky Things.**"

But then Iris started to cry
and Mummy had to go to
settle her down for her nap.

Toby was **very** cross.

"Well, if I am so good at doing things
All By Myself," he thought,
"then I will have an adventure
All By Myself too."

He packed a suitcase with Toys That Might Be Useful.
Then, when everything was ready,
he set off **All By Himself.**

Toby opened the door to
the garden All By Himself.

He climbed

down the steps

All By Himself.

And then he sat
on the swing . . .

All

By

Himself.

Toby was soon
hungry and cold.

And it turned out that
the Toys That Might
Be Useful weren't very
useful after all.

Toby didn't feel like a
Big Boy any more.

Then, just at that moment . . .

"Toby!" said Mummy.
"There you are!"

"I don't want to be a **Big Boy** and do things
All By Myself," sniffed Toby. "I want to be a baby like Iris."
"Oh, Toby," said Mummy. "You **are** my **Big Boy**.

But however big
you are, and even when
you're **all** grown up . . .

you will **always** be my baby."

"Always?" said Toby.

"Yes," said Mummy . . .